P9-DVO-318

Dear Parent:
Your child's love of reading starts here!

Every child learns to read in a different way and at his or her own speed. Some go back and forth between reading levels and read favorite books again and again. Others read through each level in order. You can help your young reader improve and become more confident by encouraging his or her own interests and abilities. From books your child reads with you to the first books he or she reads alone, there are I Can Read Books for every stage of reading:

SHARED READING
Basic language, word repetition, and whimsical illustrations, ideal for sharing with your emergent reader

BEGINNING READING
Short sentences, familiar words, and simple concepts for children eager to read on their own

READING WITH HELP
Engaging stories, longer sentences, and language play for developing readers

READING ALONE
Complex plots, challenging vocabulary, and high-interest topics for the independent reader

ADVANCED READING
Short paragraphs, chapters, and exciting themes for the perfect bridge to chapter books

I Can Read Books have introduced children to the joy of reading since 1957. Featuring award-winning authors and illustrators and a fabulous cast of beloved characters, I Can Read Books set the standard for beginning readers.

A lifetime of discovery begins with the magical words "I Can Read!"

Visit www.icanread.com for information
on enriching your child's reading experience.

I Can Read Book® is a trademark of HarperCollins Publishers.

Riff Raff Sails the High Cheese
Copyright © 2012 by HarperCollins Publishers
All rights reserved. Manufactured in China. No part of this book may be used or reproduced in any manner whatsoever without written permission except in the case of brief quotations embodied in critical articles and reviews. For information address HarperCollins Children's Books, a division of HarperCollins Publishers, 195 Broadway, New York, NY 10007.
www.icanread.com

Book design by Sean Boggs

Library of Congress catalog card number: 2013951079
ISBN 978-0-06-230510-7 (trade bdg.) — 978-0-06-230509-1 (pbk.)

14 15 16 17 18   SCP   10 9 8 7 6 5 4 3 2 1   ❖   First Edition

Riff Raff

Sails the High Cheese

Written by
Susan Schade

Pictures by
Anne Kennedy

HARPER

An Imprint of HarperCollinsPublishers

The mice pirates

stored all their loot

in a big cavern.

One day, Munster made

a terrible discovery!

4

"Captain Riff Raff!"

Munster shouted.

"Someone has stolen

our big cheese!"

The mice cried

for their lost cheese.

"We'll find it, troop,"

Riff Raff told his crew.

"We'll find our big cheese!"

"Did you lose a big cheese?"

asked a friendly voice.

It was Ali the Gator.

"I heard that somebody

saw a big cheese," Ali said.

"Somebody saw it someplace.

A place that sounds like . . .

something."

"Where?" asked Colby.

"Think! Use your brain!"

Ali thought.

"Sounds like HAT!" he said.

"Like HAT? Is it MAT? BAT? RAT?"

Cheddar asked.

"I hope it's not CAT Island,"

said Brie. The mice shivered.

"Roly-poly MAT?" asked Blue.

The crew sailed to Roly-poly MAT.

"Show yourselves!" said Riff Raff.

"Stand and deliver our big cheese!"

"What cheese?" asked the bugs.

"There's no cheese here."

The mice stopped at BAT Cave.

But the bats were all asleep.

"No cheese," they mumbled.

"No cheese."

12

"RAT sounds like HAT," said Brie.

"Let's try the RAT bunker."

"Yeah, who's afraid

of a few old rats?" Colby asked.

"At least it's not Cat Island."

"A big cheese?" asked the rat.

"We could use a nice big cheese!

Why not take us along?"

"No, thanks," said Riff Raff.

"Yo ho! Yo ho," the mice sang.

"Sail fast. Row slow.

Look high. Look low.

Do you have our cheese?

No, no, no!"

"Only one place left to look,"

said Cheddar.

"Oh no," said Swiss.

"Not CAT ISLAND!"

16

At Cat Island, they dropped anchor.

Blue and Brie swam to the shore.

"There it is!" squeaked Brie.

"I see our cheese!"

"Shush!" said Blue.

"Who's there?" someone snarled.

"Run!" whispered Blue.

"No. Not that way."

She pulled Brie back.

"To the cheese!" Brie shouted.

Riff Raff and his crew

rushed onto the island.

Five nice mice

against three fat cats!

Blue and Brie pushed the cheese.

CLUMP. It moved.

BUMP. It rolled.

SMACK!

One cat down!

"Thieves!" shouted Munster.

"Finders keepers," snarled a cat.

"Bully!" Brie yelled.

"Pip-squeak!" said a cat.

And then . . .

RATS TO THE RESCUE!

"They took our cheese,

those scary cats.

We hunted high and low.

We got it back, thanks to some rats,

and home again we go!"